MIA MAYHEM

AND THE CAT BURGLAR

#12

BY KARA WEST   ILLUSTRATED BY LEEZA HERNANDEZ

LITTLE SIMON

New York London Toronto Sydney New Delhi

This book is a work of fiction. Any references to historical events, real people, or real places are used fictitiously. Other names, characters, places, and events are products of the author's imagination, and any resemblance to actual events or places or persons, living or dead, is entirely coincidental.

LITTLE SIMON
An imprint of Simon & Schuster Children's Publishing Division
1230 Avenue of the Americas, New York, New York 10020
First Little Simon paperback edition August 2022
Copyright © 2022 by Simon & Schuster, Inc.
Also available in a Little Simon hardcover edition
All rights reserved, including the right of reproduction in whole or in part in any form.
LITTLE SIMON is a registered trademark of Simon & Schuster, Inc.,
and associated colophon is a trademark of Simon & Schuster, Inc.
For information about special discounts for bulk purchases, please contact Simon & Schuster
Special Sales at 1-866-506-1949 or business@simonandschuster.com.
The Simon & Schuster Speakers Bureau can bring authors to your live event.
For more information or to book an event contact the Simon & Schuster Speakers Bureau
at 1-866-248-3049 or visit our website at www.simonspeakers.com.
Designed by Laura Roode
Manufactured in the United States of America 0622 MTN
2 4 6 8 10 9 7 5 3 1
Library of Congress Cataloging-in-Publication Data
Names: West, Kara, author. | Hernandez, Leeza, illustrator.
Title: Mia Mayhem and the cat burglar / by Kara West ; illustrated by Leeza Hernandez.
Description: First Little Simon paperback edition. | New York : Little Simon, 2022.
Series: Mia Mayhem ; 12 | Audience: Ages 5-9. | Audience: Grades K-1.
Summary: Mia brings her cat, Chaos Macarooney, to PITS
Day, and must keep the peace between Chaos and Hugo Fast's cat,
Mr. Whiskers, before total chaos breaks out.
Identifiers: LCCN 2021053766 (print) | LCCN 2021053767 (ebook)
ISBN 9781665917216 (paperback) | ISBN 9781665917223 (hardcover)
ISBN 9781665917230 (ebook)
Subjects: CYAC: Cats—Fiction. | Ability—Fiction. | Superheroes—Fiction.
| African Americans—Fiction.
Classification: LCC PZ7.1.W43684 Mb 2021 (print) | LCC PZ7.1.W43684
(ebook) | DDC [Fic]—dc23
LC record available at https://lccn.loc.gov/2021053766
LC ebook record available at https://lccn.loc.gov/2021053767

CONTENTS

CHAPTER 1

CHAOS? WHERE ARE YOU?

A SPECIAL INVITATION

You're probably wondering why I'm running like a whirlwind through my house. As usual, I'm chasing after my cat, Chaos. When she acts up like this, it's because of one of three things: Number one, she's in the mood to make a mess; number two, she's super excited; or number three, it's both. Unlucky for me, today it's number three.

So why is she super excited? Well, you see, I just checked the mailbox, and believe it or not, there was a very official-looking invitation addressed to Chaos Macarooney . . . from none other than the PITS!

DEAR CHAOS MACAROONEY,

CONGRATULATIONS! WE'RE PLEASED TO INVITE YOU TO A SPECIAL SESSION AT THE PITS.

BEST WISHES,

Dr. Sue Perb
HEADMISTRESS

If you've never heard of the Program for In Training Superheroes, aka the PITS, here, let me explain, because this is BIG NEWS. My name is Mia Macarooney, and *I. Am. A. Superhero!* By day, I'm a regular kid at Normal Elementary School. But as soon as the bell rings, I head over to the PITS, where I go by Mia Mayhem, superhero extraordinaire!

At the PITS, I learn to use all kinds of awesome superpowers. In fact, I was supposed to be at the PITS in ten minutes! If I didn't find Chaos soon, I was going to be late.

She'd grabbed the letter out of my hands and wouldn't come out from where she was hiding.

That's why I've been running around like crazy trying to find her. I looked under the couch and even inside her favorite cubby in the kitchen. As I got up from the floor, that's when it hit me. She loves hanging out in *high* places, even if she can't get back down—don't ask me why.

So I ran to my room, and sure enough, Chaos was lounging on top of my bookshelf!

I scooped her up, grabbed the PITS letter she was sitting on, and flew back down. Chaos was *not* happy about it, but I had no time to waste.

The last time Chaos was at the PITS, absolute mayhem broke out, and my friends and I ended up chasing a pack of rowdy animals all around town! Bringing her to school sounded like a really bad idea. But my cat was smart, and I knew she could smell adventure from a mile away.

Thinking about it already made my head hurt, but I knew my mom wouldn't be thrilled to see this mess. So I stuffed the letter into my pocket and cleaned my room in a flash.

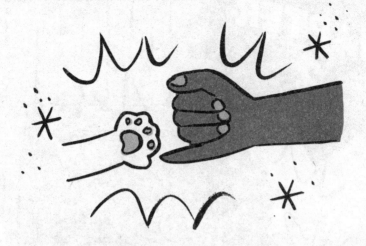

Then I made Chaos promise me she wouldn't get into more trouble. I had no idea why my crazy cat was invited to the PITS, but I needed to find out more ASAP!

9

PETS AT THE PITS?

Thanks to my superspeed, I made it to the PITS and quick-changed into my supersuit in under a minute! Then I turned the DO NOT ENTER sign and scanned myself into the building.

From the outside, the PITS looks like an old, abandoned warehouse. But on the inside, it's the coolest superhero training academy ever!

The lobby, otherwise known as the Compass, was crowded because a group of older kids was practicing advanced flying skills. I hopped on the elevator to the second floor. When I arrived, the gym was buzzing with excitement.

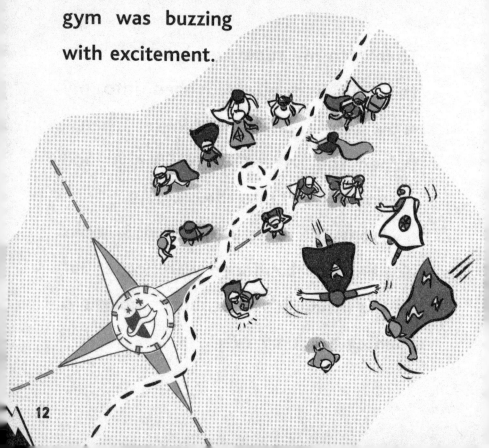

"Over here, Mia! We saved you a seat!" My friends Allie Oomph and Penn Powers waved to me from the bleachers. When I sat down, I noticed that Allie and Penn also had invitations just like mine. *What's up with these invitations?*

At that moment, Dr. Sue Perb, the headmistress, walked in, and the gym went quiet.

"Hello, students! I have exciting news!" Dr. Perb said cheerfully. "All of you should have received a special PITS invitation—you and your pets are all invited to Bring Your Pet to the PITS Day tomorrow!"

Whoa! Did you hear that? Pets at the PITS?

My friends looked over at me with big, excited smiles.

Until now, our classmate Ben Ocular, who is blind, was the only student who had a superpet sidekick who was with him at all times. What was going to happen if *everyone* brought their pets to school? Was I the only one a little bit worried?

"Mia! Isn't this awesome!" Allie gushed as we headed to flying class.

"My rabbit, Hopper, is going to love hopping around the PITS so much!"

"And I can't wait to show my mouse, Mr. Whiskers, all the cool superhero stuff that we do here," Penn chimed in. I wanted to be as excited as them, but when Chaos can really be a handful sometimes.

I got so distracted thinking about it, I could barely focus on my flying lesson. I almost crashed into Penn as he practiced his fancy midair flips! Toward the end of class, I felt even worse when I overheard Hugo Fast, the class bully, bragging about his cat, Mr. Pebbles.

"You guys are in for a treat!" Hugo said. "I have the smartest, most well-behaved cat . . . thanks to a great owner, of course!"

His friends laughed with him as they left. But my stomach fell.

Now, I *definitely* had to make sure that Chaos was on her best behavior for tomorrow's big day.

CHAPTER
3

THE PITS IS A ZOO!

The next day the PITS was as busy as a zoo! There were dogs, cats, snakes, fish, frogs, birds, hamsters, rabbits, and more! I was glad Chaos was still in her carrier for now. She can get pretty feisty, and I wasn't sure how she'd handle being around so many animals.

I saw Penn standing near a wall all by himself and walked over to him.

"Hi, Penn! Where's Mr. Whis—" But before I could finish, Penn's pet mouse, Mr. Whiskers, scampered out of a hidden pocket in Penn's supersuit and climbed onto his head! *Yikes!* I took a step back. Even though I see all kinds of animals at my dad's veterinary clinic, rodents are my least favorite.

Penn gently lifted Mr. Whiskers down from his head. "We're staying away from the crowd," Penn said. "I don't want anyone to trample Mr. Whiskers. Isn't that right, little guy?"

Penn nuzzled Mr. Whiskers's nose just as Chaos let out a loud MEOW!

MEOW! MEOW!

She was telling me she was tired of being in the carrier. I knew it wasn't fair to keep her cooped up inside, so I carefully opened the carrier door. To my surprise, instead of running off, she jumped right into my arms. I was glad that she did, because at that moment, Dr. Sue Perb walked in, along with Professor Stu Pendus.

PURR!

PURR!

25

"Hello, students and pets!" Dr. Perb said. I noticed that she was wearing her shiny star pendant that was in the shape of the Compass.

"Welcome to Bring Your Pet to the PITS Day! We'll get into the fun activities we have, but now I'll turn it over to Professor Stu Pendus."

Everyone loved Professor Stu Pendus, which wasn't surprising. He was the designer behind every PITS student's supersuit.

"Hello, everyone! I'm here because the only way to truly welcome our pets is to make them their own superhero suits!" Professor Stu Pendus said. "When I call your name, please bring your pet to get fitted. But until then, please quietly wait for your turn."

Have you ever tried to get a room full of animals to sit still? Believe me, it's *way* easier said than done. Some stopped long enough to get fitted for their suits and looked great. Others refused to get dressed altogether. Surprisingly, Chaos was very well-behaved through it all.

Right when Chaos was admiring her new suit in the mirror, I suddenly heard a loud hissing sound. Professor Stu Pendus was trying to put a suit on Hugo Fast's white Persian cat, Mr. Pebbles.

The cat wriggled, scratched, and then knocked over a box of sewing supplies before running away—with just a mask and no suit!

"My cat's too cool for a catsuit anyway," Hugo said, trying to play it off.

I decided it was best for me and Chaos to leave quickly, but before I could stop her, Chaos started hissing at Mr. Pebbles.

Uh-oh! Was Chaos just asking for trouble?

HISSSSS!

CHAPTER 4

THE HIDDEN VAULT

Once everyone was suited up, Dr. Perb divided the class into two teams. And guess what? Yours truly was chosen to be a team captain! Unfortunately, the other team captain was Hugo.

Both Hugo and I love to win, so I knew things were about to get serious. Luckily, my friends Allie, Penn, Ben, and all our pets would be my teammates.

I could tell by the frown on Hugo's face that he wasn't happy with his team, which included Mr. Pebbles, a frog, a lizard, and a fish. Hugo caught me looking at him and smirked, and I pretended not to care.

Soon Dr. Perb was ready to explain the rules of our first mission.

"Being quick and stealthy are important skills for good superheroes to have," she began. "But even the best superheroes work in teams."

My teammates gave one another a thumbs-up.

"You will have to work with your pet to get through a laser maze without setting off the alarm," Dr. Perb continued. "The first team to get to the other side and turn off the lasers will pass to the next round—good luck to all!"

With that, the room went pitch black, and a maze of bright, zigzagging lasers appeared. The crazy lights scared Chaos right away. She jumped into my arms and tried to hide under my cape.

"Don't worry, Chaos," I whispered.

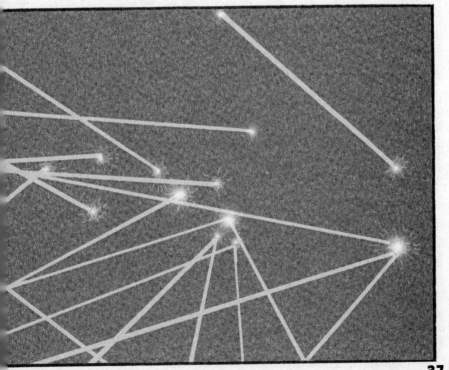

As we entered the maze, I felt a gust of wind as a girl and her bird flew by us and ran into a wall. *Whomp!* They crashed into another kid and her hairy sheepdog, who bumped into a boy and his snake. Feathers and fur were everywhere, and they all got twisted up like a huge pretzel! *BEEP BEEP BEEP!* Those teams were out.

I knew we had to get moving as carefully as possible, so I matched my steps with Chaos's. Together we flipped a row of lasers that were lined up like hurdles, climbed over a mountain-shaped laser, and even did the limbo under a laser that was low to the floor.

Ahead of us, Ben and his dog, Seeker, were in the lead. Ben was using his powerful X-ray and night vision to cut through the lasers with ease. My friends and I had also learned how to use X-ray vision, but I didn't have my special glasses with me. I was so busy admiring Ben's skill that I didn't see Hugo and Mr. Pebbles speed right past me.

I rushed to catch them, but Chaos jumped out in front of me. *MEOW!* I stopped in my tracks . . . right before I ran into a laser!

MEOW!

"Thanks for warning me, Chaos." I scooped her up and gave her a squeeze. I guess we were a good team after all.

Ben and Seeker made it to the end of the maze first, as expected. Ben pressed the special button, which turned the lasers off. Then we all watched as the door opened and revealed a hidden vault with piles and piles of gold and money!

CHAPTER 5

THE TREASURE HUNT

Chaos and I raced toward the vault. I was laser focused. *Get it? Laser? Laser maze?* Okay, never mind. Let's just say I was determined to be next. But then Hugo ran up beside me. Chaos and I ran faster, and luckily, before it closed, Penn sped into the vault right behind me with Mr. Whiskers.

Allie and Hopper and the rest of Hugo's team followed.

BZZZZ.

Dr. Perb's voice sounded over the loudspeaker.

"Congratulations to Ben Ocular and his team for finishing the maze first and winning this round!"

"Woo-hoo!" I cheered. "We did it!" I gave each of my friends a high five.

"Everyone's next mission is to find a hidden treasure map," Dr. Perb continued. "You have thirty minutes on the clock. May the best team find it!"

Right away we all began digging through piles of gold nuggets when something *super* strange happened. All the animals started sniffing the gold. And then they started *eating* it!

SNIFF, SNIFF!

RIBBIT!

"The animals are trying to eat the gold!" I yelled. "We have to do something before they get sick!"

"Hold up. Gold is metallic. It shouldn't be that easy to chew," Ben said. He scanned a gold nugget with his X-ray vision.

"Aha! Just as I thought," he cried. "The gold nuggets are actually animal treats, and this money is fake!"

That was a big relief, but we still had a treasure map to find! So my teammates and I dove into the giant piles.

We were having so much fun swimming in it at first that we, *uh*, forgot to look for the map! Before we knew it, ten minutes had passed and an alarm sounded.

The ceiling opened up, and more fake treasure poured into the vault. *Oh no!*

Now it was going to be so much harder to find the map. I had a hunch that even more treasure would be dumped soon. If we didn't find the map, we could *literally* get buried in treasure!

"We need to divide and conquer," I said to my team. "Ben, we need to use your X-ray vision to scan the piles. Penn and Allie, after Ben and Seeker scan, we need to move them out of the way."

"Great plan, Mia!" Ben, Allie, and Penn said.

Then we all started searching the vault. But out of the corner of my eye, I saw Hugo Fast watching us. *What are he and his team up to now?*

CHAPTER 6

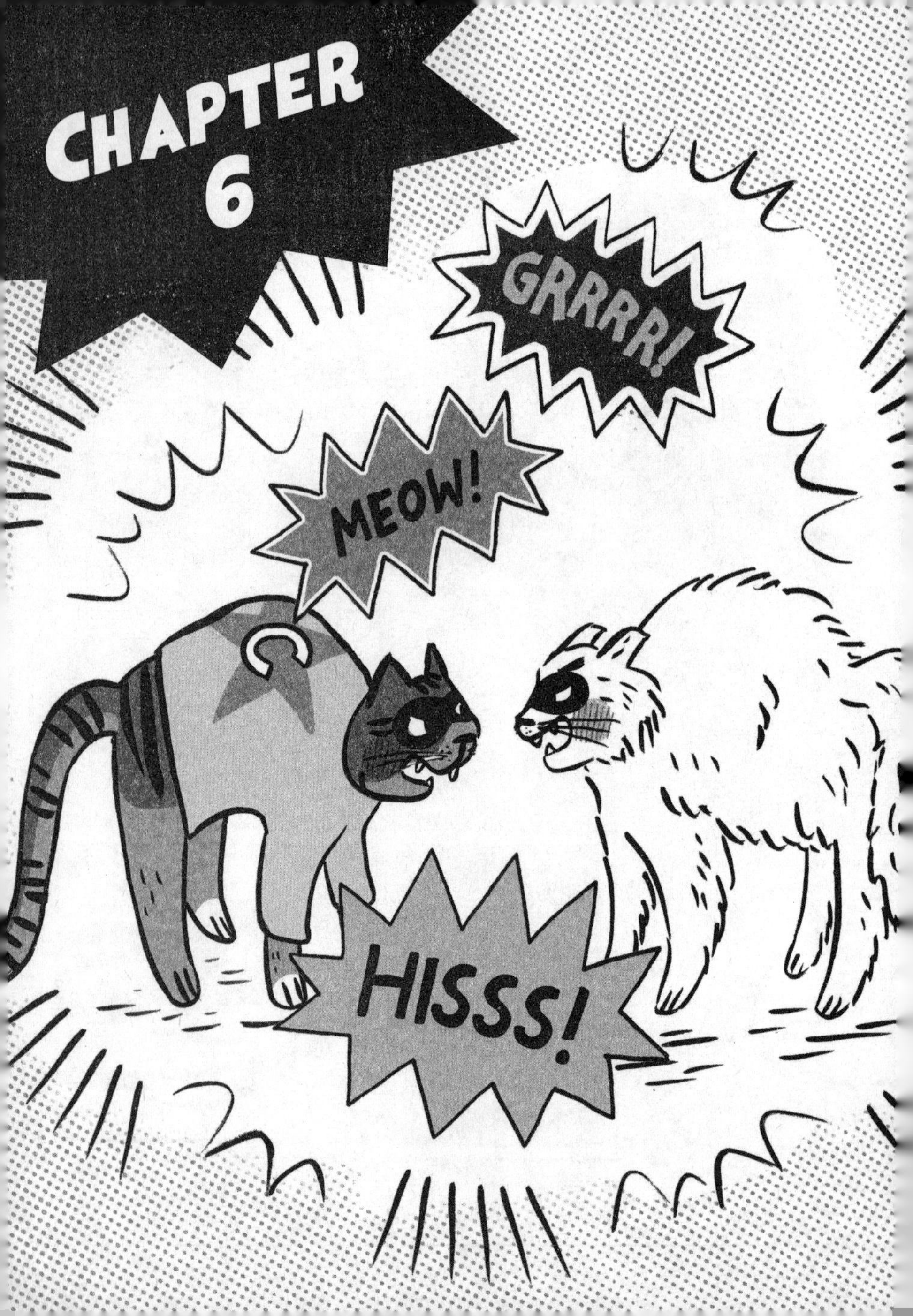

THE CAT STANDOFF

Hugo whispered something to his cranky cat, Mr. Pebbles. And before I knew it, Mr. Pebbles was headed right toward Chaos!

I tried to reach Chaos before she saw Mr. Pebbles, but I was too late. The two cats locked eyes. Chaos hissed at Mr. Pebbles, and Mr. Pebbles growled back at her. Next thing I knew, the cats were nose to nose, their backs arched.

Mr. Pebbles crouched down and leaped toward Chaos, who quickly moved out of the way. Then Chaos started pawing the ground to mark her territory. She kept hissing at Mr. Pebbles until, finally, he decided to walk away.

That seemed to put Chaos in a pretty grumpy mood.

GRRRRR!

I wanted to see if she was okay, but we only had five minutes left. There was still a lot of treasure to search through, and the map was nowhere to be found.

But then a voice rang out through the vault.

"Aha! I found it!" It was Hugo, and he was holding up his team's treasure map!

"Come on, guys! We have to find our map!" I said in a panic. But at that moment the ceiling opened, and another load of treasure started to fall. I held out my hand to try to freeze time, but nothing happened.

Darn! Now what? Hugo pushed a button on the wall, and an exit door opened. Hugo and his team rushed toward the door.

"Run ahead, Mr. Pebbles, before Mia's team catches up!" Hugo yelled. Mr. Pebbles sped off with a small bag in his mouth.

"We need to get out of here while the exit is open!" I shouted. "Let's go!" Allie, Ben, and I ran toward the door.

"Wait!" Penn shouted at the top of his lungs. "We can't leave. Mr. Whiskers is missing!"

CHAPTER 7

PETS ON THE RUN

Penn flew back and forth across the room, not sure what to do.

"Try not to worry, Penn. We'll find Mr. Whiskers," I said. "When was the last time you saw him?"

Penn thought for a moment. "He was right next to me helping me search, but after that sneaky cat, Mr. Pebbles, came by, I lost track of him."

"I saw Mr. Pebbles run off with a bag," Allie said.

"That cat was eyeing Mr. Whiskers all day. I'm sure he has something to do with this," Penn said. "We need to go after him!"

"Good idea," I agreed. "I think we should split up again. Ben and Allie, will you stay and keep looking for the treasure map here in the vault?"

"We're on it!" Allie and Ben nodded.

Then Penn, Chaos, and I ran out the door.

The exit of the vault led to a dark, empty hallway inside the PITS. Have you ever been in your school at night, when there's no one around? Trust me, it's pretty creepy. I heard footsteps in the distance, so Penn and I followed the sound . . . until we realized it was Hugo!

Hugo spotted us over his shoulder and ran even faster.

"He's running away!" Penn cried. "He must have something to hide!"

So Penn and I used superspeed to catch and stop him.

"Hey! Where's my mouse?" Penn demanded.

"What are you talking about? I don't know anything about your silly mouse," Hugo said with a smirk.

"Well, I'm sure your cat does," Penn said, giving Hugo an angry stare.

"We saw Mr. Pebbles run off with a bag. What was in it?" I asked.

Hugo shrugged. "You could ask him yourself . . . if you can find him."

"What do you mean, *find him*?"

Then it hit me! Hugo was in the hallway all by himself.

"I don't know where he is. He took
off before I could see where he went,"
Hugo said. Then his face turned serious.

So, you may know by now that Hugo Fast is not exactly my favorite person. I was not super-excited about helping him find his cat. But I did want to make sure that Penn's mouse, Mr. Whiskers, was not in danger. Plus, having animals lost inside the PITS was not a good situation. At all.

CHAPTER 8

CHAOS BRINGS CHAOS

"Okay, Hugo. We'll help on one condition: no sneaky tricks."

"Me? Sneaky? Never!" Hugo cried.

"Do we have a deal, or what?" I asked.

"Oh all right, it's a deal," Hugo agreed.

Just then, Chaos jumped into my arms and nuzzled my nose, which gave me a *super*-brilliant idea.

Chaos had an excellent sense of smell. She could use this power to help find the lost pets.

After I explained my plan, Chaos sniffed Hugo to pick up his cat's scent. When we followed Chaos to the cafeteria, she started making a giant mess!

Before we knew it, pots and pans were flying everywhere, globs of food were splattered over the counters, and puddles of spilled milk and juice covered the floor. Hugo, Penn, and I did our best to clean up the mess, but we could barely keep up.

In typical Chaos fashion, that was just the beginning. She knocked over chairs and desks in classrooms, pulled almost all the books off the shelves in the library. She even spilled all the sand out of the punching bag in the gym.

Finally, Chaos led us to Dr. Sue Perb's office, and I was surprised to see Ben and Allie in front of the office door.

"Hey, guys! How did you find us?" I asked.

PURR!

PURR!

"We just followed Chaos's mess. That made it super easy to figure out where you guys were headed," Allie said with a smile.

I filled Ben and Allie in on our search for Mr. Pebbles and Mr. Whiskers and then walked over to the office door, which was already open a crack. It looked dark in the room, but I knocked anyway just to be sure Dr. Perb wasn't inside. No answer.

"The coast is clear," I whispered to Penn, Hugo, Allie, and Ben, then pushed open the door.

Dr. Perb's office looked like a hurricane had just stormed through it! *Oh no!* We had to fix this or we'd be in big trouble.

But before I could start to clean, Chaos jumped up onto the couch and began meowing loudly.

Penn, Hugo, Allie, Ben, and I rushed over to see what was wrong.

And that's when we saw that Mr. Pebbles was behind the couch with the bag he'd taken from the vault!

"Mr. Pebbles!" Hugo cried, and rushed over to scoop Mr. Pebbles into his arms.

"Glad you and your cat are reunited. But I still want to see what's in that bag," Penn demanded.

He picked up the bag and gently emptied the contents on the floor. A bunch of fake-gold animal treats tumbled out of the bag, along with . . . Mr. Whiskers!

CHAPTER 9

WHO'S TO BLAME?

"Mr. Whiskers! I thought you were gone forever!" Penn picked up his mouse but then quickly turned to Hugo.

"I knew your cat had something to do with this!"

"Oh yeah?" Hugo stepped forward like he was about to challenge Penn.

But at that very moment, Dr. Perb walked into the room.

"What on earth happened to my office?" she gasped.

"It was Hugo's fault!" I yelled. "His cat has been acting weird all day. Mr. Pebbles started a fight with Chaos."

"It was Mia's fault!" Hugo yelled back. "And her messy cat was the one that started the fight!"

Dr. Perb held up her hands. "Mia! Hugo! Quiet please."

We stopped yelling. Then Dr. Perb made us talk one at a time.

"His cat kidnapped Penn's mouse, Mr. Whiskers, from the vault. Plus, he stole a bag of gold!" I blurted out.

"That's not true!" Hugo insisted. "Mr. Pebbles just wanted some extra treats. I'm sure he had no idea the mouse was inside!"

"Well, Mr. Pebbles was wrong for running off with the bag," Dr. Perb said. "But it doesn't seem like Mr. Pebbles is that interested in Mr. Whiskers at all," she continued. We looked down to see Mr. Pebbles busily eating the animal treats from the bag.

I had to admit Dr. Perb had a point, *but still*!

"Dr. Perb, I still think Mr. Pebbles is up to something!" I insisted.

"No, your cat, Chaos, is definitely up to something!" Hugo shot back.

"That's enough. All pets have been found, so no harm done," Dr. Perb said firmly. "Every superhero needs to learn how to admit when they are wrong and apologize with grace."

Hmph. I didn't want to say sorry, but I also knew that what Dr. Perb had said was true. My mom always told me that great superheroes knew when to do the right thing. And I, Mia Mayhem, am a *great* superhero!

"Sorry, Hugo, for accusing Mr. Pebbles of kidnapping Mr. Whiskers before I had all the facts," I mumbled.

"And I'm sorry for sending Mr. Pebbles over to distract you in the vault earlier. And sorry that your mouse was in the bag," Hugo said to me and Penn. We all nodded and shook hands.

"I think our cats have said sorry to each other, too." I laughed and pointed to Chaos and Mr. Pebbles, who were curled up next to each other on the couch.

"Great job, both of you," Dr. Perb said to me and Hugo, then asked all of us to head back to the gym. As we walked toward the door, I saw Dr. Perb take off her Compass pendant and place it in a box on her desk.

THE SUPER PET SECRET

A few minutes after we got to the gym, Dr. Perb walked in.

"I hope that everyone had a great time today," Dr. Perb said.

Most kids cheered and applauded, but I let out a sigh of relief.

"Unfortunately," Dr. Perb continued, "there will not be a winner this year. Due to some trouble between teams, we will not be keeping score."

A loud groan went around the room.
I could tell some kids were disappointed
that there wasn't going to be a winner.

And I felt extra bad because I knew Dr. Perb had canceled all the points because of what had happened with me and Hugo.

As the rest of the class started to leave, Dr. Perb called my name.

"Mia! May I speak with you for a moment?" Dr. Perb asked.

Uh-oh! Am I somehow in trouble again? I thought.

GULP!

I walked as slowly as possible over to Dr. Perb.

"Yes, Dr. Perb?"

"Mia, I wanted to share some exciting news." Dr. Perb smiled. *Exciting news? Whew!*

"What's that?" I asked.

"Well, to tell you the truth, the Bring Your Pet to the PITS Day was actually an undercover trial to see if any of our students' pets have what it takes to be a superhero sidekick," she said. "And Chaos passed the test!"

109

"Wh . . . what does that mean?" I asked, confused.

"Nothing will change for now. Chaos should just keep living her best cat life," Dr. Perb said. "But we've been watching her, and her speed, agility, and quick thinking are top-notch superpet material."

My mouth dropped to the floor. My crazy cat was super . . . just like me!

"Now, she will need special training eventually," Dr. Perb continued. "So if you get another invitation in the future, you'll know what it's for."

I nodded eagerly. That didn't sound too hard.

"Thanks, Dr. Perb," I said, giving a shy smile.

"Oh, that's not all, Mia," Dr. Perb replied. "Before you and Hugo can go home, you have to clean up the mess your pets made in my office. *Without* using any superpowers."

I wasn't looking forward to it, but I knew it was fair. So a little while later, Hugo and I walked together to Dr. Perb's office. When we opened the door, the office was even worse than when we'd left earlier—thanks to Chaos and Mr. Pebbles, who had clearly joined forces to create the biggest mess ever!

115

I finally cornered Chaos behind the desk and picked her up to calm her down. That was when I noticed that the box with Dr. Perb's special Compass pendant, which she had left on her desk earlier . . . was gone!

Chaos and Mr. Pebbles were the only ones in the room after we left, which could mean one of three things:

Number one: that Mr. Pebbles wasn't so innocent. Had he meant to kidnap Mr. Whiskers after all?

Or number two: Chaos was somehow involved, and both cats were guilty.

Or number three: Neither cat was the culprit, and there was a more dangerous burglar out on the prowl.

If it was option number three, maybe Chaos would get a chance to be a superhero sidekick sooner than I thought.

But for now, I had a gigantic mess to take care of, so that would have to be a super cat adventure for another time. . . .